Check List...

- ☐ camera
- ☐ compass
- ☐ boots
- ☐ socks
- ☐ net

Stanley is busy getting his things ready, this week his family are going with Lily's family for a camping holiday. "Can you see what Stanley has on his checklist?" Take a look around his room see if he has everything.

camera	appareil
compass	boussole
boots	bottes
socks	chaussettes
net	filet

Stanley's four sisters are also packing, let's see what they have got ready to take.

four pairs of wellies	quatre paires de bottes de pluie
four sweaters	quatre pull-overs
four nets	quatre filets

Mum and dad have got the sleeping bags ready. There are seven sleeping bags, (seven - sept). One for each family member. The sleeping bags are yellow (jaune - yellow).

seven	sept
yellow	jaune

Finally, the car is packed, Stanley's family are all excited. Let's see if Lily's family are ready to go.

Lily's family are all packed, they just have to load the car up. They have two brown suitcases and a box full of food. Lily's dad has a lovely red hat.

two	deux
brown	marron
red	rouge
hat	chapeau

"All ready to go, come on everyone, in the cars". Lily's family have a red car, Stanley's family have an orange car.

red	rouge
orange	orange

They seem to be lost, Stanley's mum says to pull over so she can look at the map on her phone. (map - plan)

"Mum! Dad!" shouts Stanley, "here's the camping site."

mum	mère
dad	père
camping	camping

Stanley's and Lily's parents go into the booking office to pay for the campsite and get a map of the area.

campsite	terrain de camping
map	plan

The tents are up. Stanley's tent is orange, with blue and white stripes and Lily's tent is yellow.

orange	orange
blue	bleu
white	blanc
yellow	jaune

It has been a busy day, the parents have made a picnic and got the deck chairs out to relax.

How many tents can you see? _____

What colour are the deck chairs? _____

What colour are the parasols? _____

Everyone has settled down for the night, tomorrow they are all going down to the river, "Good night Lily" shouts Stanley.

"Bonne nuit Lily", shouts Stanley.
"Bonne nuit Stanley", shouts Lily.

| goodnight | bonne nuit |

The families have walked to the river, Lily is pushing her sister on a bike.

river	rivière
bike	vélo

The two boys rowed across the river in a boat to Stanley and Lily. One of the boys has fallen over in the boat which makes Lily laugh. The boys are twins.

twin	jumeau
twins	jumeaux
boat	bateau
boy	garçon

"Hello" shouts Stanley as the boat reaches them, "Bonjour", came the reply from the boys. "Are you French?" asks Lily, "Oui" reply the boys.

"Parlez-vous français?" the boys ask Stanley and Lily. "Oui, un peu" says Lily. (Lily says yes, a little).

hello	bonjour
boys	garçons
do you speak French?	parlez-vous français?
boat	bateau
yes	oui
a little	un peu

Stanley asks the boys, "Quel est votre nom?" "What is your name?"

"Je m'appelle Jade" says one boy, the other boy replies "Je m'appelle Pierre".

Pierre asks Lily, "What is your name?"
Lily replies "Je m'appelle Lily" then Stanley says "Je m'appelle Stanley".

what is your name?	quel est votre nom?
my name is _____	je m'appelle _____
quel est votre nom?	je m'appelle _____
parlez-vous français?	

Jade is asking you what is your name, can you fill in the blank spaces? Now he's asking do you speak French, how will you reply? (Oui - yes)   (non - no)

Pierre asks Stanley and Lily if they want to have a go at fishing. "Yes please" shout Stanley and Lily together. (oui, s'il vous plaît) (yes, please)

Stanley's dad brings the children their nets and a bucket.

Lily's dads sit on the bench to watch the children fishing

un
deux
trois
quatre
cinq
six
sept
huit
neuf
dix

one
two
three
four
five
six
seven
eight
nine
ten

Stanley and Lily play with the twins in their boat. Pierre and Jade are saying a number in French and Lily and Stanley have to guess the number in English.

fill in the blank spaces with the numbers in French.

one	two	three	four	five
six	seven	eight	nine	ten

"Wow" shout the children, "Look at the rainbow", Lily's sister says it's pretty. "Let me and Lily say the colours" says Stanley, "Then you tell us what they are in French Pierre and Jade".

red	rouge
orange	orange
yellow	jaune
green	vert
blue	bleu
indigo	indigo
violet	violet

Can you put the colours in English?

rouge	
orange	
jaune	
vert	
bleu	
indigo	
violet	

rainbow - arc en ciel

"what is rainbow in French" Pierre?

"arc en ciel"

"how many colours are in the rainbow?"

"sept couleurs"

rainbow	arc en ciel
colours	couleurs
seven	sept

Pierre and Jade's dad has come to take his sons home, he tells the boys to say goodbye to their friends. "Goodbye Lily and Stanley" (au revoir)

Stanley's Mum and sisters have also come to collect Stanley and Lily.

"Have you had a nice day?" asks Stanley's Mum,
"Yes thank you, Mum" says Stanley.

The parents have made a picnic for tea.

Stanley's family go to the showers to clean up after their busy day.

It's bedtime, Stanley and Lily are sleeping in their sleeping bags outside under the stars.

time for bed	à dormir
stars	étoiles
sleeping bag	sac de couchage

Today, the families have decided to stay at the campsite and have a barbecue.

campsite	terrain de camping
barbecue	barbecue

The families are having a game of football, although Lily's sister wants to play badminton. The footballs are black and white.

black	noir
white	blanc

What a fun day the families are having. This is a wheelbarrow race, it's Stanley's family racing Lily's family.

"Faster Daddy" shouts Lily. (race - course)

"Three, two, one go" shouts Stanley's mum.

three	trois
two	deux
one	un

The parents have arranged egg and spoon races for the children. Everyone is having fun.

egg	œuf
spoon	cuillère
parents	parents

Everyone is ready for bed after another fun filled day, but while everyone is sleeping, the wildlife come out to play.

A lot of people have left the campsite today. The families decide to treat the children to ice creams and ice pops.

| ice cream | glace |

They are spending the day at a summer camp so the children can join in the activities.

| children | enfants |

It's been a long day, the children are tired so they catch the little train back to the campsite. "All aboard" shouts Dad, laughing.

| train | train |

The children are tucked up in bed, so the parents enjoy a well earned break to themselves.

Stanley's Mum and Lily's Dads are having a clean up in the tents.

cleaning	ménage
dust	poussière
broom	balai

Stanley's Dad is keeping an eye on the children as they enjoy the paddling pool.

paddling pool	pataugeoire
duck	canard

Stanley and Lily's families all go to the restaurant for tea, the holiday is almost over.

restaurant	restaurant

merci mère
et père

merci
pères

As everyone gets ready for bed, Stanley and Lily are busy gathering flowers and making thank you cards for their parents.

thank you	merci
mum and dad	mère et père
dads	pères

Next day, Stanley and his Dad are playing golf. They have both got new caps.

golf	golf
cap	casquette

Stanley's Mum and Lily's dads have taken the girls to a play area.

mum	mère
dad	père
girls	filles

tir à la corde (tug of war)

It's the last night of the holiday, everyone plays at tug of war. (tir à la corde) (tug of war)

Everyone has packed up ready for the drive home.

"au revoir" (goodbye) they all say to each other.

Home sweet home, "let's go inside and make a drink" says Daddy.

"Come on children, let's get inside and ready for bed" says Dad.

Stanley's sisters are in bed, Stanley and his parents are having a nice cup of tea and some biscuits.

"Brush your teeth Stanley and wash your hands and face."

Stanley's Dad is getting ready for a nice soak in the bath.

"Goodnight Stanley" says his mum, **"Sweet dreams"** **"Love you to the moon and back"**.

"I love you Mum" says Stanley, bonne nuit, (good night)

I love you	je t'aime
good night	bonne nuit

apple _ _ _ _ _

ant _ _ _

angel _ _ _ _ _

airplane _ _ _ _ _ _ _ _

Bb

ball

ball

_ _ _ _ _

bat

_ _ _ _

Cc

cat

_ _ _ _

coat

_ _ _ _ _

cat

dog _ _ _

desk _ _ _ _

doll _ _ _ _

dragon _ _ _ _ _ _

How many?

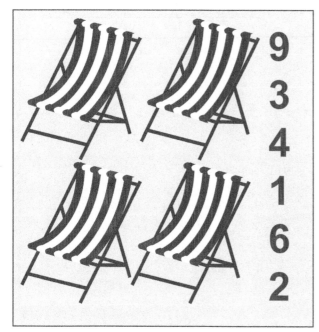

9
3
4
1
6
2

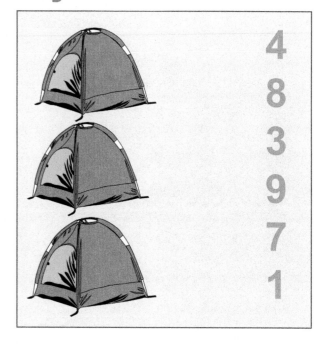

4
8
3
9
7
1

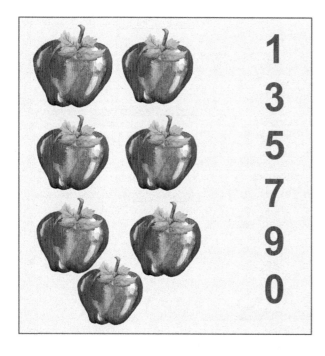

1
3
5
7
9
0

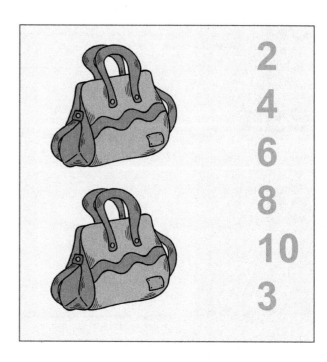

2
4
6
8
10
3

elephant _ _ _ _ _ _ _ _

egg _ _ _

elbow _ _ _ _ _

envelope _ _ _ _ _ _ _ _

How many?

how many boys?	
how many bells?	
how many Stanleys?	
how many Lilys?	

Ff

frog

frog _ _ _ _ _

fluffy_ _ _ _ _ _ _

Gg

Goat

goat _ _ _ _ _   gecko _ _ _ _ _ _

greenhouse _ _ _ _ _ _ _ _ _ _

un one	deux two	trois three	quatre four
cinq five	six six	sept seven	nuit eight
neut nine	dix ten	3	7
10	5	1	9
2	6	8	4

Can you match the numbers?

hat _ _ _

house _ _ _ _ _

igloo _ _ _ _ _

ice _ _ _

jam _ _ _

jug _ _ _

kangaroo _ _ _ _ _ _ _ _

kite _ _ _ _

Ll

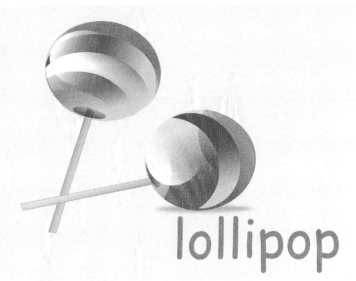

lollipop

lollipop _____

llama _____

mouse _____

month _____

nest _ _ _ _ _
nut _ _ _ _

orange _ _ _ _ _ _ _

ocean _ _ _ _ _ _

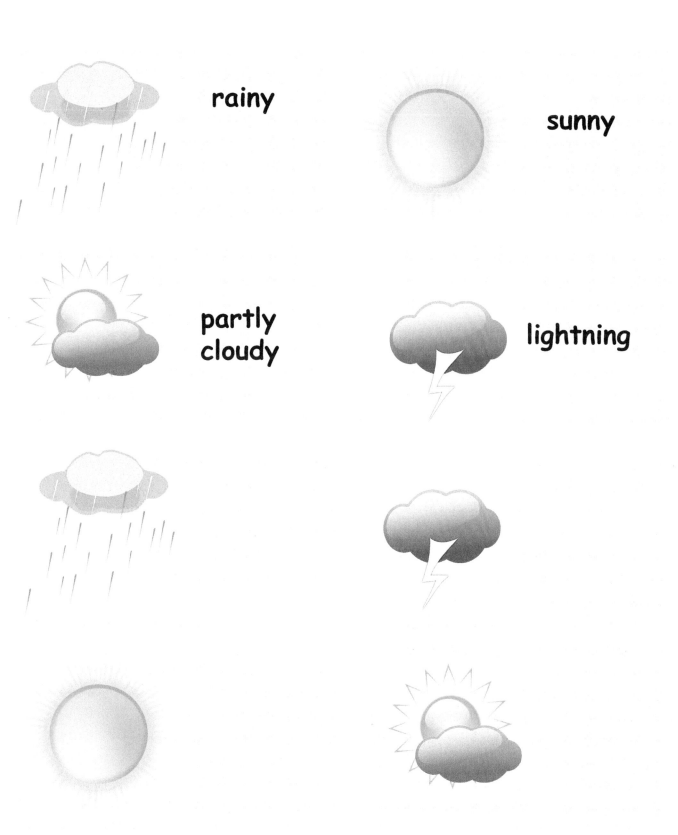

rainy

sunny

partly
cloudy

lightning

Write in the weather

pig _ _ _

penguin _ _ _ _ _ _ _

queen _ _ _ _ _

quarter _ _ _ _ _ _ _

rocket _ _ _ _ _ _

racquet _ _ _ _ _ _ _

sun _ _ _

solar _ _ _ _ _

happy

laughing

sad

angry

Fill in the emotions

turtle _ _ _ _ _ _ _

toy _ _ _

Uu

umbrella

umbrella _ _ _ _ _ _ _ _

utensils _ _ _ _ _ _ _ _

lemon

bananas

pineapple

apple

Write the names of each fruit

1 + 3 =
3 + 3 =

5
4
8
6
2

2 + 4 =
5 + 2 =

7
9
6
2
5

0 + 1 =
1 + 8 =

2
9
7
1
8

8 + 1 =
4 + 5 =

7
9
3
6
4

Write the answers to the sums

vase _ _ _ _ _ _

vulcan _ _ _ _ _ _

wagon _ _ _ _ _ _

wheel _ _ _ _ _ _

x ray _ _ _ _ _

xylophone _ _ _ _ _ _ _ _ _

yellow _ _ _ _ _ _

yacht _ _ _ _ _

zebra _ _ _ _ _ _

zig zag _ _ _ _ _ _ _

Printed in Great Britain
by Amazon